# Curious, Furious Chipmunk

by JANE THAYER [o Pseud.]
Catherine Woolley

illustrated by Seymour Fleishman

William Morrow & Company
New York

With thanks to Charlotte and John for their wonderful window

Charlie Chipmunk stood on tiptoe,
and he made very mad sounds.
He was furious!

Until now life had been good in the woods.

Charlie had his underground house.

He could always find nuts to eat.

For company he had

Mrs. Squirrel, Mrs. Rabbit, Raccoon,

old Woodchuck, Deer, and the birds.
Suddenly all was changed.
Some people named Newman
had wandered into the woods
and decided to build a house.

Now a bulldozer was bulldozing.
There was such a commotion that
Mrs. Squirrel, Mrs. Rabbit, Raccoon,
old Woodchuck, Deer, and the birds
had moved out, bag and baggage.
"This neighborhood is ruined,"
Mrs. Squirrel snapped.

Charlie was furious enough to move away,
but he was so curious that he had to stay.
The bulldozer bulldozed trees
to make a clearing.
Charlie sat outside his underground house,
peeked from behind a tree,
or stood on tiptoe in the grass,
to see what was going on.

Drills began to drill,
hammers began to hammer.
The Newmans' house took shape.

Every night, when the workmen left,
Charlie, still furious,
inspected it inside and out.

At last the house was finished.
Charlie inspected the outside
and tried his best to get inside.
He scampered around the wide window
that looked out on the clearing,
furious because he couldn't see in.
Down the narrow road
rumbled a furniture van.
The Newmans moved in.
Charlie was furiously furious,
but of course he was curious
so he still stayed around.

The very first day
the Newmans were there
Charlie watched Mrs. Newman
scatter corn in the clearing
and put out birdseed.
His eyes bulged, his nose twitched.
He had never seen so much food.
He ran around,
sniffing from various angles,
and wherever he sniffed
the food smelled delicious.
"But it's dangerous," said Charlie to himself.

He stayed at the edge of the clearing
and stood on tiptoe
to see what was going on.
He wasn't the only curious one, he noticed.
Mrs. Newman was usually looking out.
Charlie made mad sounds.
One morning Charlie was up early.
No one was stirring.
Suddenly he felt more curious than furious.
He had to investigate that house.
He was on the doorstep, investigating,
when the door opened
and out came Mr. Newman.

Charlie was so startled
he couldn't move for a moment.
"Good morning!" said Mr. Newman.
Charlie raced away
and ducked into his house,
his heart hammering.
When he felt calmer he came out.
Mr. Newman stood on the doorstep.
"Come on. Breakfast is ready," he called.
Charlie ducked back into his hole.
He didn't go near the house again that day.
But after a night's sleep
he began to feel curious again.
And, when he came out and stood on tiptoe,
he saw that the door
of the Newman house was open.
"Aha!" said Charlie.
He scampered to the door.
He peeked inside.

Charlie's nose began to twitch
as he smelled something delicious.
Right before his nose
lay some scattered kernels of corn.
Charlie was hungry, and he forgot
the Newmans' food was dangerous.
He scampered through the door.
He stuffed his left cheek full of corn.
He stuffed his right cheek full.
He came to something like a tree trunk,
and he sniffed corn on top.
His right cheek would hold
three more kernels, he figured,
so he scampered up the trunk.
Here was some corn, all right.
Charlie had stored two kernels
in his right cheek,
when suddenly a horrible suspicion
crept over him.

He looked up
and found himself face to face
with Mr. Newman.
He had climbed Mr. Newman's leg
to Mr. Newman's knee,
and he was eating corn
out of Mr. Newman's hand.
Mr. Newman
looked mighty pleased.

Charlie fell off
Mr. Newman's lap,
raced across the floor,
flew out the door,
rushed through the clearing,
and ducked into his hole.
He put the corn in his storehouse,
sat down to calm his nerves,
and thought about
the horrible adventure he had just had.
He was furious at Mr. Newman
for fooling him.
"But you're too curious, Charlie!"
he told himself severely.
"You will come
to no good end."

He went to sleep that night muttering
"I'm furious, I'm furious.
But I can't *help* being curious!"
He woke up next morning hungry again.
He could still taste
the delicious corn
he had eaten the day before.
Suddenly he thought,
I believe today

I'm curious enough to try
that food she puts out.
He scampered boldly into the clearing.
It seemed perfectly safe.
He scampered farther.
Perfectly safe.
He sampled some corn.
It tasted wonderful,
and Charlie stuffed both cheeks.

He rushed home
and stored the corn in his storehouse.
Charlie began to lead a busy life.
He ate and he ate.
He found he could stuff
fifteen kernels of corn into his left cheek
and sixteen into his right.
He filled his storehouse up to the ceiling.
He dug a new storehouse.
He dug little holes
here and there
under the leaves,
in case he wanted
a snack.

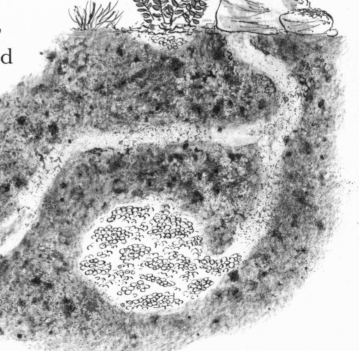

He often noticed
Mrs. Newman looking out.
He pretended he didn't see her.
Sometimes, before he went to sleep,
Charlie thought of his old friends,
Mrs. Squirrel and the others,
and wondered where they were.
Too bad they went away, he thought.
Autumn came,
and Charlie worked longer and longer hours
storing food for winter.

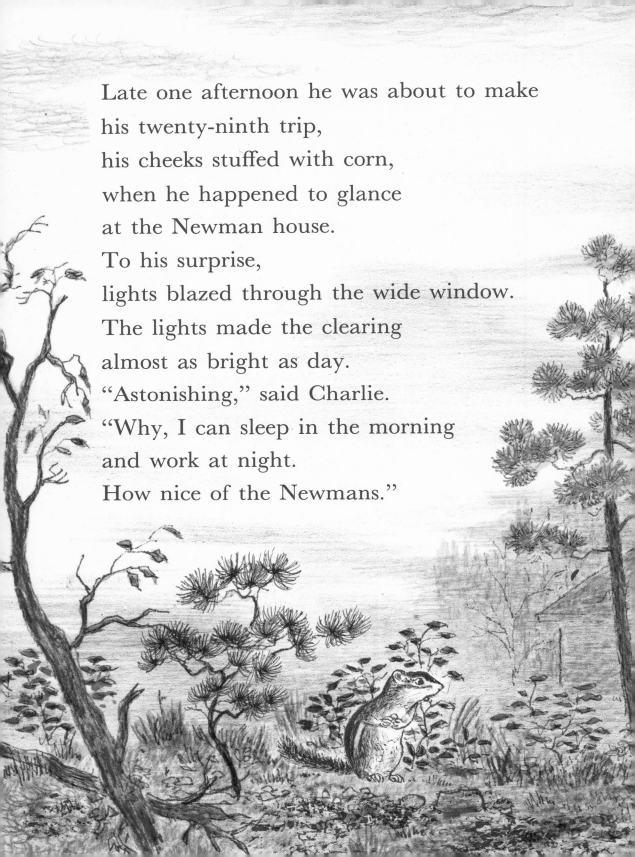

Late one afternoon he was about to make
his twenty-ninth trip,
his cheeks stuffed with corn,
when he happened to glance
at the Newman house.
To his surprise,
lights blazed through the wide window.
The lights made the clearing
almost as bright as day.
"Astonishing," said Charlie.
"Why, I can sleep in the morning
and work at night.
How nice of the Newmans."

He began to enjoy a late snooze
in the morning.
It was pleasant
to pull up the blankets,
because mornings were frosty now.
Leaves were fluttering down
from the trees.

One day Charlie
had got himself out of bed,
and was carrying
thirty-one kernels of corn
to his newest storehouse,
when he heard, quite close,

*Bang!*

*Bang, bang!*

The hunters are out, he thought.
He raced home, his heart hammering.
Quivering underground,
he soon heard a different bang.
He peeked fearfully out,
and he saw that Mr. Newman
had banged the door
and was coming across the clearing.
Mr. Newman wore such a thundery look
that Charlie ducked back.

When he peeked again,
Mr. Newman was tramping through the woods
toward the edge of his property.
Charlie was so curious
that even though he was scared
he crept out to see what was happening.
"Private property!"
roared Mr. Newman
at the hunters.
"No hunting here,
*if you please!*"

The hunters departed.
Mr. Newman went tramping home.
"Thank goodness," said Charlie.
And he thought of his old friends.
They were probably
quaking with fear of the hunters
somewhere in the woods.
Charlie hurried out
and stood on tiptoe
at the edge of the woods.
"Hello, everybody!" he shouted.
"No hunters on our property!
Come on home!"

He saw them coming, bag and baggage.
Mrs. Squirrel and her two little girls.
Mrs. Rabbit,
six boys and twenty-seven girls.
Raccoon, Mrs. Raccoon, small Raccoons.
And old Woodchuck.
Far in the background, Deer.
With them flew
the chickadees, the blue jays, and the quail.
"Follow me!" yelled Charlie.

They reached the clearing at dusk.
They hungrily sniffed the food.
The Squirrels scampered
into the open first.
The Rabbits and Raccoons followed,
and Woodchuck lumbered after them.
Deer lingered shyly.

Charlie was delighted
to have everybody home.
They were all busily eating
when lights blazed from the window.
"Isn't this fine?" said Charlie proudly.
"Just as light as day!"
"Astonishing," said Mrs. Squirrel.
"This neighborhood is quite nice now."

Then Charlie glanced at the window again,
and his eyes bulged.
He could see
Mrs. Newman getting dinner,

Mr. Newman reading the paper,
candlelight on the table,
firelight on the hearth,
and other interesting things.

He made very pleased sounds.
He stood on tiptoe
to look and look and look.
He forgot to eat, but that was all right,
because he had two million,
four hundred ninety-six thousand,
seven hundred and twenty-eight
kernels of corn
in his various storehouses.
He wasn't a bit furious
at Mr. and Mrs. Newman now.
But he was
just as curious
as ever.

2645